I0548305

STEVE HUTCHISON

CREEPYPASTA
TOWN

Copyright © 2024 by Steve Hutchison

All rights reserved. No part of this publication may be reproduced, distributed, or transmitted in any form or by any means, including photocopying, recording, or other electronic or mechanical methods, without the prior written permission of the publisher, except in the case of brief quotations used for purposes of review, commentary, or scholarly analysis.

First Edition, 2024
ISBN-13: 978-1778872877

Published by Tales of Terror
Website: https://terror.ca
Social Media: @terrorca

Steve Hutchison – steve@shade.ca
Bookstores and wholesalers: Please contact books@terror.ca

PREFACE

Welcome to the shadowy heart of Creepypasta Town. Within these pages lie 10 of my most spine-chilling tales, each crafted to drag you into a realm of terror and twisted imagination. What began as fleeting whispers on the internet has grown into fully realized nightmares designed to grip you from the first word to the last.

Each story is paired with evocative illustrations, drawing you deeper into a world where the ordinary twists into the grotesque. From unsettling psychological horrors to chilling supernatural encounters, these tales will linger in your mind long after the final page, making you question what lies just beyond the edges of reality.

Prepare yourself for a plunge into darkness, where nothing is as it seems and fear takes many shapes. May these stories haunt you as much as they haunted me. Proceed if you dare—and enjoy the ride.

Steve Hutchison

STORIES

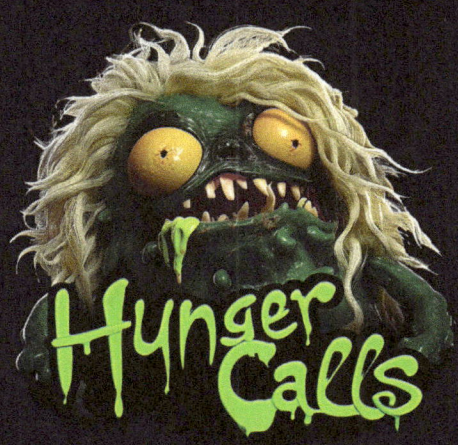

Hunger Calls

I'd been living in that building for about six months when the problems started. At first, it seemed like any other apartment complex—quiet, nondescript, the kind of place you settle into when you're working shifts and just need somewhere to sleep. But then my landlord, Mr. Carrington, began popping up more often. His complaints about my music and TV volume were always annoying, but I wasn't breaking any rules. I worked nights, and as far as I was concerned, I had every right to exist, even at 3 a.m.

Still, Mr. Carrington was persistent. He'd knock on my door, muttering about noise complaints from the other tenants. And when I tried to bring up the fact that someone might be stealing my mail, he'd dismiss it with a wave of his hand. "You're imagining things," he'd say, like I was just some paranoid tenant. I couldn't stand him.

One day, after a particularly exhausting shift, I found myself in the lobby, once again arguing with Mr. Carrington. I'd given him a list of things to repair, a few leaky faucets and broken tiles, and his response? He threatened to raise my rent to cover the cost of repairs. I stared at him, my mind racing. He was always so dismissive, but I was done with it. I told him I was entitled to make noise, that I paid rent like everyone else, and

he gave me that usual condescending look, telling me he had better things to do than check the building's cameras.

It was 4 a.m. when I got back to my apartment. I hadn't slept all night, and now I couldn't shake the feeling that something was off. Mr. Carrington was supposed to come by the next day to fix the plumbing, but he'd canceled on me last week, and I had no idea what he might do today. He always gave me such a broad window of time that it ruined my whole day. I wanted to be there when he came, just in case.

Then, as I was standing in my kitchen, trying to distract myself from the creeping anxiety, something caught my eye. At first, it was just a flicker—movement, out of the corner of my eye. I turned quickly, expecting to see a mouse or some other small animal. But no, there was something by the sink.

By the sink, there was something. A small, grotesque creature, crouching like a twisted shadow. Its eyes gleamed, dark and wet, and for a moment, Darrell couldn't even process what he was seeing. It was unlike anything he had ever seen before—a creature with too few limbs and a body that shifted as if it weren't meant to be seen in the light. Its form flickered, an unnatural shape that seemed to bend with the room's shadows.

For a long moment, neither of us moved. Then, it spoke.

It wasn't loud, but its voice was piercing, almost a whisper in the back of my mind. "Come closer," it said, its tone high-pitched and unsettling.

I froze, my heart thumping in my chest. I didn't know what I expected, but it sure wasn't... that. My mind raced. The creature's voice was familiar, too—so oddly familiar, like it had been watching me for longer than I wanted to admit.

I grabbed a knife from the counter, keeping it in my hand like a shield, but I didn't move toward the creature. It didn't seem to care. "I come from the sewers," it continued, its body twitching

as it spoke. "I've seen your landlord. He's been taking your things, you know. When you're not home, he goes through your apartment, taking whatever he can."

The realization hit me like a punch to the gut. My missing clothes, the strange gaps in my inventory—of course. But I didn't know what to think. I was too stunned to even respond.

The creature continued, its voice a low hum. "I've been living in this building for a hundred years. I know everyone here. I watch. And I tell stories. I only ask for a little food in return."

A chill ran down my spine, but I didn't want to show fear. I could feel it there, though, simmering under my skin, as I cautiously lowered the knife. "Food?" I asked, still not entirely sure I wasn't hallucinating.

"Yes," it purred. "Something to fill me up. Something good. Then, I will tell you... everything."

I wasn't sure what it wanted, but I couldn't bring myself to leave. The knife felt too light in my hand, my body too heavy. I turned, almost mechanically, and prepared a plate of vegetables. I'd been hoping for a quiet night, a night of sleep, but instead, I had a strange creature in my kitchen, asking for food. And I had to know what it knew about Mr. Carrington.

The monster ate slowly, savoring each bite like it was its last. Its form expanded, growing slowly with each mouthful. Its hair—if you could call it that—stretched, wriggling like it was alive, and the creature's form seemed to stretch with it, becoming bulkier and more terrifying as it fed.

"More," it demanded after a while, its voice insistent. "I want meat."

I hesitated. My stomach churned at the thought of feeding it meat, but I didn't have a choice. I added the meat to the plate and pushed it closer, my eyes locked on the creature. It was

growing faster now, its body inching closer to the size of a small dog, its limbs thickening and stretching unnaturally as it devoured the food.

"Tell me about her," I muttered, glancing nervously down the hall at the woman who'd moved in a few weeks ago. The one with the soft laugh, the one who always smiled at me. "The neighbor at the end of the hall."

The creature grinned, its eyes glittering. "She's... very interesting," it said. "But I'm going to need more to eat before I can tell you about her."

My thoughts swirled. What else did this thing know? What else had it seen? I didn't know how long I could keep feeding it. But its voice was almost hypnotic, and soon I was feeding it more, asking questions, desperate for answers. As the hours ticked by, I began to ask about myself. The creature's response was chilling. "You want to know, don't you? I know everything. And to hear it, you'll need to feed me more."

By the time I realized what it was asking, it was already too late.

The monster continued to grow, and with each new meal, it expanded faster and faster. It had become larger than I could have imagined. And when it finally told me everything, when it spoke of the tenants and their dark secrets, I knew I had to act. The monster was insatiable, demanding more, pushing for... something worse.

I could feel the weight of my decision as I made my way to the landlord's apartment, knife in hand. What I did next changed everything.

But when the monster devoured the landlord's flesh, it grew faster than Darrell had ever expected. Its limbs stretched and twisted, its body swelling like a balloon. The apartment around him began to crack and groan, the walls buckling under the

weight of its growth. It towered over Darrell, its form expanding with every breath. The ground shook as the creature surged, growing larger and larger, until it smashed through the ceiling, rampaging through the building.

Darrell stood frozen in place, mesmerized by the creature's monstrous transformation. What had been a small, grotesque thing was now a towering, hulking force, filling the entire apartment. It tore through walls and doors as if they were paper, its limbs thrashing wildly. The air vibrated with the sound of the creature's growth, a deep, guttural rumble that seemed to reverberate from the very core of the building. It wasn't just growing; it was consuming the space itself, twisting reality around it. The building groaned, the foundations shuddering, as if the structure was fighting against the weight of this unnatural force.

And still, it grew.

The creature's growth didn't slow; it continued to expand, stretching and contorting, growing in height and size with each passing moment. Darrell's mind couldn't comprehend the scale of it—this thing that had started as a tiny creature, now turning into a grotesque titan. The air was thick with the scent of decay as it tore through the building, plaster, wood, and glass raining down around him. The very ground beneath his feet trembled with the power of its growth. With a final, violent crash, it burst through the building's outer walls, sending debris flying like confetti. The force of its emergence was so powerful that the building seemed to collapse inward, leaving nothing but a crumpled heap of what used to be his home.

The creature stood in the open air now, towering above the city like a force of nature, its form still expanding, stretching toward the heavens. It was no longer just a being—it was a colossal, destructive entity. As it rampaged through the streets, everything in its path was consumed. Buildings crumbled to dust, cars were crushed, and people scattered, screaming, running for their lives. But there was nowhere to hide. The

creature's hunger was insatiable, devouring everything in its path. Its size, its appetite, seemed to know no bounds. With each step, it grew, consuming not just flesh but the very fabric of reality itself.

Darrell, standing in the wreckage of his apartment, watched as the monster continued its rampage. His mind was numb, but there was something deep inside him, something dark and twisted, that felt satisfaction. The landlord was gone, yes, but so was everything else. The city—his life—was vanishing in front of him, crumbling like a house of cards. But what was worse, what gnawed at him now, was the realization that this creature wasn't just feeding on the world—it was feeding on the very essence of existence. It wasn't just devouring flesh. It was consuming the fabric of reality itself, the core of everything he knew.

And still, it grew.

It was unstoppable now. Every person it consumed, every building it crushed, seemed to fuel its monstrous growth. It wasn't just destroying; it was transforming the world around it. Darrell watched helplessly as the creature's shadow fell over the city, its hulking form blotting out the sky, casting every-thing in darkness. It had become more than a monster. It had become a force of nature, a living nightmare, bent on reducing everything to dust.

He realized too late that it was his fault. The monster had fed on his choices, his fears, his desperation. It had become what he had unwittingly summoned. It had always been in that building, lurking, waiting for the right moment to break free. And now that moment had come. Darrell had opened the door to this nightmare, and now, there was no escape. The city, his life, was lost. And the creature would continue to grow, devouring everything until there was nothing left.

It had started small. But now? Now, it was a god.

Clown Convention

It was supposed to be a simple day out. Janis, my girlfriend of five years, had been trying to help me confront my fear of clowns. A clown convention wasn't exactly my idea of fun, but she insisted it would be good for me. I couldn't say no to her. She'd always been there for me, and I didn't want to let her down. So, despite the unease sitting heavy in my chest, I agreed.

When we arrived, the convention center was even more garish than I had feared. Balloons floated everywhere, tethered to brightly painted stands. The building was decked out in colors that clashed in a deliberate, jarring way—red, yellow, aqua, pink. It smelled like cotton candy and popcorn, but beneath the sugary scent, there was something else, something sharp and chemical that made my stomach churn. Everywhere I turned, people in clown costumes filled the space, their laughter and chatter bouncing off the walls in a cacophony that was almost dizzying.

Janis reached into her bag and pulled out two red rubber clown noses. "Here," she said brightly, pressing one into my hand. "Let's put these on. It'll be fun!"

I hesitated. The idea of wearing the clown nose felt absurd, almost humiliating. But I didn't want to ruin her day. She

looked so excited, so hopeful. Reluctantly, I placed the rubber nose over my own. It felt strange and smelled faintly of plastic, but Janis beamed at me, her enthusiasm momentarily soothing my nerves.

She stepped back, pulling her phone from her pocket. "Smile!" she said, raising the camera.

I tried. I really did. But my lips refused to curve upward. Instead, my mind filled with memories I had worked hard to bury—the hospital basement, the flickering fluorescent lights, the clown I had seen as a child. Its painted face had twisted into something monstrous, something not of this world. My parents had written it off as a nightmare, but I knew better. I'd never been able to forget.

Janis frowned slightly, lowering her phone. "Hey, you okay?" she asked, her voice gentle.

"Yeah, I'm fine," I lied. "Just... taking it all in."

She smiled again and slipped her hand into mine. "It's going to be fun, I promise. Let's just walk around for a bit. You'll see, it's not so bad."

I nodded, not trusting myself to speak. We moved through the entrance, past an enormous painted archway that read "Welcome to the Clownvention!" in bold, cheerful letters. Inside, the space was packed with people. Clowns juggled, performed tricks, and posed for pictures with kids and adults alike. The air buzzed with noise—laughter, music, chatter—but it all felt oppressive, like it was pressing down on me from every angle.

A small clown approached us, taking our tickets with a flourish. It didn't speak, just stared at me with dark, gleaming eyes before stepping aside. The exchange was brief, but it left me unsettled. I couldn't pinpoint why, exactly, but I felt cold.

Janis seemed oblivious. She tugged me forward, pointing out various attractions and booths. She was in her element, completely unbothered by the swirling chaos around us. I envied her ease. For me, every clown we passed seemed to bring back flashes of that basement. I kept catching glimpses of painted faces that lingered just a little too long on me, as if they knew something I didn't.

We wandered deeper into the convention, past booths selling clown-themed merchandise and food stalls offering brightly colored snacks. The deeper we went, the stranger everything felt. The air was thick, almost humid, and the laughter seemed to grow louder, more distorted. I tried to focus on Janis, on her cheerful voice and reassuring presence, but it was like the walls were closing in.

At one point, Janis stopped in front of a funhouse maze. "Let's go in!" she said, already stepping toward the entrance.

"Do we have to?" I asked, my voice tight. The idea of wandering through mirrored halls and distorted spaces filled me with dread.

She turned back to me, her expression softening. "Come on, it's just for fun. You'll be fine. I'm right here."

I didn't want to disappoint her, so I followed. The maze was a disorienting nightmare of bright lights and warped reflections. Every turn brought more confusion, and every distorted image of myself felt like a mockery. The laughter followed us in, echoing off the mirrored walls, growing louder and more unnatural with each step.

I started to lose track of time. It felt like we'd been wandering for hours, though it was probably only minutes. Janis stayed ahead of me, her pace quick, her movements purposeful. I tried to keep up, but the further we went, the more uneasy I became. Each reflection of her seemed subtly different, like the mirrors were distorting more than just the space. I noticed her smile in

one reflection seemed sharper than it should have been, like the glass had exaggerated its width and brightness.

Finally, we emerged from the maze into a narrow hallway. The walls were painted in faded carnival stripes, and the air smelled cloyingly sweet. It was quieter here, the noise from the main hall reduced to a distant hum. For a moment, I felt a small flicker of relief.

But then Janis turned to me, her expression unreadable. "Wait here," she said. "I'll be right back."

Before I could respond, she disappeared around a corner. I stood there, alone, the hallway stretching out endlessly in both directions. The air felt heavier now, and the distant hum of laughter seemed to shift, becoming something darker, more sinister. I wanted to call out to her, to tell her to come back, but my voice caught in my throat.

As I waited, the lights above flickered, casting strange shadows on the walls. My unease grew with each passing second. The hallway felt alive, like it was watching me, waiting for something to happen. And then, faintly, I heard the giggling.

It started soft, almost imperceptible, but it grew louder, echoing off the walls. It wasn't joyful laughter—it was something else entirely, something cold and mocking.

My skin prickled as the sound surrounded me, and I realized it wasn't coming from the hallway. It was coming from everywhere.

I turned, desperate to find Janis, but the hallway seemed longer now, stretching into darkness. My heart pounded in my chest as I took a hesitant step forward.

And then I saw her.

She was standing at the end of the hallway, her back to me. Relief washed over me for a brief moment. "Janis!" I called, my voice trembling.

She didn't respond. Slowly, she turned to face me, and my breath caught in my throat. Her face was painted like a clown's, her lips painted into a wide, red smile.

Her eyes gleamed with an intensity I didn't recognize. She tilted her head, her expression unreadable.

"Janis?" I whispered, taking a step back. "What's going on?"

Her painted smile widened. "Oh, you poor thing," she said, her voice sweet but laced with something darker. "You never figured it out, did you?"

"Figured what out?" My voice cracked. "What are you talking about?"

She took a step toward me, her movements slow and deliberate. "You've been so afraid of clowns your whole life," she said. "But it wasn't clowns you were afraid of. It was me."

I stared at her, my mind racing. "What are you saying? This isn't funny, Janis."

She laughed, and the sound was unlike anything I'd ever heard. It was sharp and cold, a sound that cut through me. "It's not funny," she said, her voice low and twisted. "It's the truth."

Her words hung in the air, heavy and suffocating. My stomach turned as the realization hit me. This wasn't the Janis I knew. Or maybe it never had been.

The pieces fell into place, and I understood. She had been leading me here, guiding me into this nightmare. It wasn't a coincidence. None of it was.

"You're one of them," I whispered, my voice barely audible.

Her painted smile widened even further, splitting her face unnaturally. "I've always been one of them," she said, her voice
echoing through the hallway. "And now, you're mine."

The laughter swelled around me, filling the space, drowning
out everything else. The world seemed to tilt, the hallway
stretching and twisting as her painted face loomed closer.

I wanted to run, to escape, but my legs wouldn't move. I was
rooted to the spot, as if the air itself had turned to stone around
me.

And as the darkness closed in, her laughter was the last thing I
heard.

KillShake

Louis could hear the rumble of the delivery truck pulling up the street, his heart racing with anticipation. It was finally here. After weeks of late-night scrolling, reading glowing reviews, and convincing himself this was the answer, SlimShake had arrived. The perfect solution. No more diets. No more endless hours at the gym. Just one shake and bam—a body that was always just out of reach. Lose weight fast, it promised. It's almost too easy, they said.

Perfect timing. Louis glanced over his shoulder, making sure his mom's car wasn't in the driveway. She wouldn't be back for at least an hour. A perfect window. He grabbed the package with a grin, cradling it like a prized possession. This was it. No more struggle. No more failures.

He dashed into his room, shutting the door behind him with excitement buzzing in his veins. He tore open the box, practically vibrating with eagerness. Inside, nestled among crinkly packaging, was the familiar bright white packet. It screamed efficiency with its stark, clean design—SlimShake emblazoned in bold, no-nonsense letters. The smiling image of a perfect person stared back at him. He couldn't wait to look like them.

The powder inside was a flawless vanilla hue, so smooth, so perfect. The packet promised no added sugar, only pure results.

Louis grinned, tearing open the first pouch and inhaling deeply. Sweet, a little synthetic, but intoxicating. Vanilla, maybe? There was something else too, but he couldn't place it. Maybe it's just part of the magic, he thought.

He followed the instructions with a fervor, mixing the powder into a glass of milk. But then his eyes fell on a basket of fresh strawberries in the fridge—an impulse. Health, right? He tossed a handful into the blender, blending it all together into a creamy, indulgent concoction that turned a rich shade of pink. It was so thick, so frothy, it could've been straight out of some Instagram influencer's smoothie bowl.

Louis couldn't resist. He took the first sip. The taste was heavenly—smooth, creamy, with just the right amount of sweetness. But then there was that aftertaste. It was faint, but familiar. Something... wrong. It lingered at the back of his throat, elusive and unsettling, but he shrugged it off. Not bad at all. He settled on the couch, the glass now empty beside him. His stomach gave a low growl. Not the usual hunger. This was different. A deep, rumbling discomfort that seemed to vibrate through his body.

"Whoa," Louis muttered, pressing a hand to his gut. The cramps hit almost instantly—sharp, twisting pains that wracked his insides. His stomach lurched as if something inside him was alive, stretching and contorting.

He barely made it to the bathroom before vomiting violently into the toilet. A pink spray splattered the floor, staining the porcelain. He could barely see through the haze of nausea, but he felt something crawling under his skin—a pulsing, twisting pressure.

"Oh no... oh no..." he muttered, panicking as the mess spread across the bathroom floor. His mom would kill him if she saw this. He grabbed the mop, scrubbing frantically, but something in his gut made him stop. The scale.

Exhausted, sweaty, and shaking, Louis stumbled back into his room. His curiosity gnawed at him, like a tickle in his brain he couldn't ignore. He stepped onto the scale, hesitated, then looked. The numbers blinked back at him—eight pounds lighter.

"What the...?" Louis whispered, stepping off, then back on again. The same numbers blinked back at him, relentless. Impossible. He hadn't even worked out. He'd just downed a shake, spent the day on the couch. But the numbers didn't lie. Maybe it worked, he thought. Maybe this thing actually worked.

His stomach growled again, but now, it was different. Louder. More insistent. A deep, vibrating growl that made his bones ache. The cramps came back, stronger this time, more intense. Before he could react, his body spasmed violently. He collapsed to the floor, retching uncontrollably.

The world spun. He could barely hear his own thoughts over the deafening thrum inside him. And then... something. A faint, pulsing sound. Was it his heartbeat? Or something deeper? Inside of him?

In a fevered haze, he thought he felt it. Something moving... inside.

It was a quiet evening when Donna, Louis' mom, pulled into the driveway, humming softly to herself. Bingo night had been good—enough winnings to cover groceries for the week. But something felt off. As she parked the car and glanced up at the house, she noticed a faint glow leaking from Louis' upstairs window. That wasn't right. He usually kept all the lights on, especially when he was home alone. The house felt unnervingly silent.

"Louis? I'm home!" she called, her voice breaking the stillness as she closed the door behind her.

No answer.

The silence was... thick. The air felt too heavy, like it was pressing in on her. It was cloying, sweet in a way that made her stomach churn. The smell—it wasn't normal. Vanilla, sure, but there was something under it, something sour, something... wrong.

Donna wrinkled her nose, scanning the room. A faint glimmer caught her eye. She looked down.

Pink.

Pink? Her mind tried to register it. At first, she thought it was some spilled juice, or cleaning product—but no. It was too vivid, too deliberate. Too... unnatural. Her pulse quickened. She hesitated, then took a step forward, her eyes following the droplets. Pink. Droplets. A trail. They weren't random. They were in a line, guiding her somewhere. A sense of dread settled deep in her gut. She didn't want to follow it, but something was pulling her forward.

With each step, the scent grew stronger, more intoxicating. Her head began to swim as the smell wrapped around her like a heavy fog. By the time she reached the stairs, the air was thick—almost unbearable. She forced herself to breathe through her mouth, but it was everywhere.

"Louis?" she called again, louder now. Her voice trembled.

Still, no answer.

The trail of pink led her into the hallway. The droplets turned to streaks, then to splashes, like the walls themselves were being consumed. The hallway felt... wrong now. The vibrant, almost fluorescent pink pulsed in the dim light, as though it were alive. It reminded her of milkshake. Only this was something much darker. Something alive.

At the top of the stairs, the door to Louis' room was slightly ajar, a ghostly glow spilling out, casting long shadows that seemed

to stretch unnaturally. Donna's heart began to hammer in her chest. She didn't want to see what was behind that door, but she knew she had to.

She pushed it open, and the sight froze her.

Louis was lying on his back, nearly lifeless, sprawled across his bed. His skin was ashen, pulled taut over the bones of his face. His eyes—wide, unblinking—stared blankly at the ceiling, but there was no life in them. No recognition. His body looked thinner than she'd ever seen him. Almost skeletal.

And standing over him... that.

It wasn't human, not entirely. It was made of what looked like twisted intestines, pulsing and writhing as though they were alive. It shimmered with a grotesque, fleshy pink glow, like something straight out of a nightmare. It had no eyes, but Donna could feel its gaze—no, not a gaze. Something worse. It pierced through her.

The creature's body rippled and shifted unnervingly, trying to adjust to its horrifying new form. It reached down, its slimy arm-like appendage extending towards Louis, touching his leg. With a sickening squelch, his leg dissolved into the thing. Like sludge. Consumed.

"No," Donna gasped, her voice barely a whisper. The words caught in her throat.

The creature grew, reshaping itself, pulling more of Louis' body into it, merging his flesh with its own. It almost looked human now—its proportions eerily similar to her son's. But the face... the face that emerged was no longer Louis. It was something else, something twisted.

"Louis?" Donna whispered, but it came out as a strangled sob.

The creature's mouth opened, but what emerged wasn't a voice. It was a wet, gurgling sound—something crawling from the depths of a swamp. It moved, jerky and awkward, like a newborn learning to walk, toward Donna.

She backed away, but her legs wouldn't move. She was frozen in place, rooted to the spot. The creature lunged at her with impossible speed, its slimy arm grabbing her wrist. An icy, unnatural grip. A strange sensation crawled beneath her skin, as though something was trying to merge with her.

"Let me go!" she screamed, wrenching her arm free. She stumbled back into the hallway, but the walls seemed to close in on her, pulsing with the rhythm of her heartbeat.

Panicked, she ran down the stairs, nearly tripping as the house seemed to sway around her. She burst through the front door, running faster than she ever had before, not stopping until she reached the neighbor's house.

She pounded on the door, breathless, shaking.

"Please, help!" she begged.

But when the door finally opened, there was no one there. Nothing at all.

When the authorities arrived hours later, they found the house empty. No sign of Louis. No sign of Donna. Only an empty SlimShake packet, lying on the floor, its logo smiling up at them like a cruel mockery.

A faint, almost imperceptible trail of pink sludge led to Louis' room. But there were no further clues.

And somewhere, another delivery truck rolled down another street.

Meteor Crawl

Dale Thompson was no stranger to long nights alone. A veteran trucker, he had spent more than a decade hauling freight across the country, living for the quiet moments in between jobs. His lakeside cabin in rural Montana was his sanctuary, a place to unwind and escape the endless miles of highway. Normally, the nights there were tranquil, with only the occasional hoot of an owl or the gentle lapping of water against the shore. But tonight was far from normal.

The lake, usually a silent mirror to the vast sky above, shimmered with a peculiar sense of tension. The wind had stopped entirely, and the air felt thick, charged. As Dale leaned back on his couch, sipping a warm beer, he caught sight of a streak of light cutting through the inky sky. It wasn't a shooting star. This was brighter, more intense, and its trajectory ended in a blinding flash beyond the lake, deep in the forest. The earth beneath his boots seemed to tremble faintly, as if the world itself had taken notice.

Curiosity, coupled with a growing sense of unease, gnawed at him. Meteors were rare in these parts, but this one—there was something off about it. Something he couldn't quite put his finger on. The way it fell, like a piece of fire torn from the sky, made his heart race. It wasn't a typical meteor; it was too deliberate, too purposeful. It didn't take long for Dale to grab a

flashlight, a pair of work gloves, and a wheelbarrow. The trek around the lake was quiet, eerily so. Even the wind seemed to hold its breath as he moved through the shadows of towering pines. The trees, normally a familiar sight, now loomed like dark sentinels, watching his every step, their branches stretching unnaturally towards him.

By the time Dale reached the crater, his pulse was hammering in his chest. The meteor sat at the center like a glowing heart, pulsing faintly in shades of pink, red, and yellow. It wasn't a rock in any familiar sense. It looked more like polished glass, smooth and strangely symmetrical, reflecting the eerie glow of the night sky. He crouched, his gloved fingers hesitating inches above its surface. The warmth radiating from it was almost comforting, and yet it carried a faint hum that set his teeth on edge, like an electric current just beneath the surface.

With great care, Dale lifted the meteor and placed it in the wheelbarrow. The colors seemed to intensify as he did so, almost as if responding to his touch. He didn't linger; the sooner he could get back to his cabin, the better. The path back was rough, and he kept glancing over his shoulder, plagued by the unsettling sense that he was being watched. The forest, once alive with nocturnal sounds, seemed unnaturally silent now, and every shadow seemed to move just out of the corner of his eye. The stillness was oppressive, heavy, like the earth itself was holding its breath.

At home, Dale set the meteor on the living room table, encasing it under a glass bell jar. The room felt strangely colder, as if the air had shifted in the presence of the mysterious object. He sat back on the couch, laptop in hand, eager to make sense of the bizarre find. A reverse image search turned up nothing. Articles about meteors spoke of iron, nickel, and rare metals, not glowing rocks that pulsed like living things. As the hours passed, the glow of the meteor seemed to seep into the room, casting shifting shadows that played tricks on his mind. The patterns on the walls seemed alive, dancing and shifting with a rhythm that was faintly unsettling, as if whispering secrets

he couldn't quite hear. His eyes kept flicking to the jar, unable to tear himself away.

The darkness outside deepened as the night stretched on. His stomach growled, but the thought of food seemed distant, almost irrelevant. Finally, he stumbled upon a cryptic article titled "The Mystery of Color-Cycling Meteorites." His pulse quickened as he clicked the link, but his excitement was short-lived. The page redirected to an error message. Frustration boiled within him, mingling with a strange sense of foreboding. Outside, the lake was still, its surface like a mirror reflecting the crescent moon. But within the cabin, something stirred. A faint sound broke through the silence—a soft scratching, almost like nails on wood. The noise seemed to come from somewhere near his living room table.

Unnoticed by Dale, a small, glowing centipede emerged from the base of the table. Its body mirrored the meteor's shifting colors, a living echo of the stone. It moved cautiously, almost tentatively, as if exploring its surroundings. Across the room, another centipede emerged, then another. They were drawn to the meteor like moths to a flame. As they gathered, their movement seemed almost synchronized, their bodies wriggling in eerie unison, a dance of chitinous limbs and shimmering hues. Dale still hadn't noticed them, too absorbed in his search for answers. He rubbed his eyes, trying to focus. The glow of the meteor pulsed, its light casting strange, elongated shadows on the walls.

The faint sound of scratching grew louder, more distinct. Skittering. Scratching. He tensed, his mind jumping to mice or squirrels, unwelcome but familiar guests in the aging cabin. But this wasn't the sound of small animals. No, this was something different. Something more deliberate, more insidious. The hairs on the back of his neck stood on end as the noise seemed to follow him.

In the bathroom, the sound followed him. Standing at the sink, he glanced at the mirror and froze. Behind him, just at the edge

of the frame, something moved—a flicker of light and shadow. He spun around, but the room was empty. The unease in his chest deepened as he returned to the living room, his every step feeling heavier, as if the very air had thickened, pressing against his chest. His eyes darted nervously around the room. He thought he heard a faint whisper, but dismissed it as the wind—or maybe just his imagination playing tricks on him.

The meteor's glow had intensified, casting the room in a surreal, otherworldly light. The shadows seemed to deepen in response, drawing closer. Dale decided to distract himself with his virtual reality headset, hoping a few rounds of gaming would settle his nerves. The headset flickered to life, transporting him into a simulated world of digital landscapes and neon corridors. The digital escape felt fragile, though, as if the real world was still pressing in from all sides, clawing at his consciousness, bending the very fabric of reality.

What he didn't see was the army of glowing centipedes creeping closer. They covered the walls and ceiling, their synchronized movements almost hypnotic. At the center of the swarm was a massive centipede, far larger than the others. Its segmented body shimmered with the same colors as the meteor, and its face bore an unsettling resemblance to Dale's own. Its mandibles twitched as it observed him, its multifaceted eyes gleaming with an intelligence that was deeply unnatural. The centipede's gaze seemed to pierce through Dale, as if it could see not just his body but his very soul.

Dale moved blindly through his living room, narrowly avoiding the creatures by sheer luck. The largest centipede descended slowly from the ceiling, its legs clicking against the glass bell jar. It studied the meteor for a moment before lifting the jar with ease, cradling the glowing rock like a precious jewel.

The faint hiss of the creature broke through Dale's VR session. He yanked off the headset, his heart stopping at the sight before him. The enormous centipede loomed over the table, the meteor glowing brightly in its grasp. Its gaze locked onto Dale, and in

that instant, he felt something terrifyingly intimate—a connection, as though the creature wasn't just observing him but understanding him, reading his every thought. It was as if it had known him for years, had watched him from the moment he first touched the stone.

The room erupted in chaos. The swarm surged forward, their glowing bodies casting dizzying patterns across the walls. Dale stumbled backward, grabbing a nearby wrench and swinging wildly. The metallic clangs echoed through the cabin, but the centipedes were relentless. They didn't attack directly; instead, they seemed focused on the meteor, moving in perfect unison around their massive leader, their bodies wriggling and undulating like a living, breathing mass.

The meteor's glow intensified, its colors cycling faster and faster until they blended into a blinding white. Dale shielded his eyes, the light burning through his eyelids. The heat was unbearable, a searing presence that seemed to touch his very soul. When it finally dimmed, the meteor was no longer a smooth stone but a jagged crystal, pulsing with an almost heartbeat-like rhythm. The centipedes scattered, retreating into the shadows, their glowing bodies fading into the darkness.

Dale's head spun. He could feel the air in the room shift, thickening, as though it had been charged with something ancient. For a moment, everything was still. Then came the sound—a low, guttural hum that seemed to come from within the crystal itself, vibrating through the floor and into Dale's chest. His pulse quickened, his breath shallow. The room felt alive with energy, as though the very walls were closing in on him.

The creature that had once been the leader of the centipedes now hovered in the center of the room. Its body was no longer just an insect; it had grown, morphing into something far more menacing. It was almost humanoid now, its segmented legs tapering into delicate, almost skeletal arms. The face—it was Dale's face, distorted, twisted, and grinning with a grotesque mockery of his own smile. The skin was slick with a strange,

iridescent sheen, the eyes—those eyes—burning with an alien intelligence that made his stomach twist.

In a voice that was both his own and not, it spoke, the words chilling him to his core. "You've touched it, Dale. You've woken it. Now, it's part of you, as you are part of it."

Dale couldn't move. His legs locked in place as the room spun around him. The walls seemed to bend and twist, the very air vibrating with the creature's presence. The floor beneath him felt like it was giving way, warping into an abyss that threatened to swallow him whole. The darkness seemed to grow, taking shape, pressing closer. He wanted to scream, but his mouth was dry, and his body refused to obey.

The last thing he saw before the light overwhelmed him was the centipede creature, its multifaceted eyes gleaming with anticipation. Its smile widened, sharp mandibles clicking as it reached for him.

When Dale awoke, hours—or was it days?—later, he was alone again. The cabin was quiet, save for the distant ripple of the lake. But something had changed. The air felt thick, oppressive, like the very space around him had been altered, twisted. And when he looked in the mirror, he saw it: the same eyes staring back at him, glowing faintly, shifting in strange, pulsing patterns. The last traces of his own humanity, it seemed, were gone. The creature—whatever it was—had left its mark.

And as the days passed, the skies above Montana began to glow, cycling through strange colors. Whatever had come from the stars, it wasn't finished with Dale yet. It was just getting started.

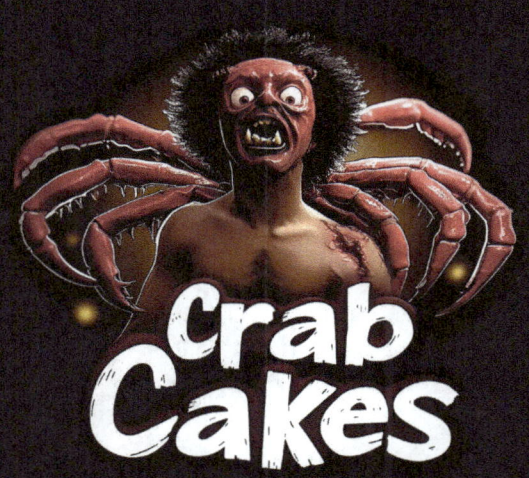

Crab Cakes

There was nothing like game night. Every Friday, Minjay and Junho would turn off the world and dive into their retro game console, a dusty but beloved relic from their high school days. Tonight's pick was Broken Wings, an old-school side-scroller with pixelated landscapes and frustratingly difficult bosses. It had been years since they'd last played it, but that only made the experience sweeter.

Minjay set the box of crab cakes down on the coffee table with a triumphant grin. "Here we go," he said, waving his hand theatrically over the food like a magician presenting a trick. "Fresh from Arirang Delights. Everyone says their crab cakes are to die for."

Junho snorted. "I'll be the judge of that. But if it's better than the stuff from Gogi Palace, I'll forgive you for making me wait an hour to eat."

The two of them plopped onto the couch, grabbed their chop-sticks, and dug in. The crab cakes were, in a word, divine. The texture was perfect, crispy on the outside and buttery soft on the inside. The flavor—a balance of sweet crab meat and subtle spices—was enough to make them both stop mid-bite to look at each other with raised eyebrows.

"Okay," Junho said after swallowing. "You win. These are incredible."

Minjay laughed. "Told you. Arirang never misses."

The box was soon emptied, greasy chopsticks abandoned on the table as they fired up the console. The startup chime of Broken Wings filled the small apartment, a nostalgic sound that made both of them grin.

For the next twenty minutes, the world outside their screen ceased to exist. They dodged enemies, collected power-ups, and shouted in triumph and frustration. The crab cakes were forgotten, their memory lingering only in the faint, savory aroma still wafting from the empty box.

But then Junho groaned.

At first, Minjay didn't notice. He was too focused on navigating a particularly tricky section of the game. But when Junho groaned again, louder this time, Minjay glanced over.

"You good?" he asked.

Junho was hunched over, his controller abandoned on the couch beside him. One hand clutched his stomach, and his face was pale and glistening with sweat.

"I don't know," Junho muttered. "My stomach... it's killing me. Like, cramps or something."

Minjay frowned. "Food poisoning? Maybe the crab cakes..."

"I don't think so," Junho said, his voice strained. "This feels... worse. Different."

Before Minjay could respond, Junho let out a strangled cry. His back arched, and his hands shot up to clutch at his neck as if something invisible were choking him.

"Junho!" Minjay scrambled off the couch, knocking over his controller in his haste. "Hey, what's happening? Are you choking? Should I call someone?"

Junho didn't answer. He was too busy screaming. His skin, once smooth and lightly tanned, began to ripple and bulge in unnatural ways. Minjay watched in horror as something—no, things—erupted from Junho's back. At first, they looked like long, sharp bones, but as they grew and unfolded, it became horrifyingly clear that they were something else entirely: pincers.

"Oh my God," Minjay whispered, stumbling backward. "Junho... what is this?"

Junho's screams turned guttural, almost inhuman, as his face began to change. His jaw jutted forward, elongating into a grotesque, chitinous snout. His eyes swelled and darkened, the whites disappearing entirely. And his hands... oh, his hands. They twisted and contorted, fingers merging and hardening until they, too, became pincers.

The transformation wasn't instantaneous. It was grotesquely slow, as if Junho's body was fighting back. Bones cracked audibly, his joints bending at impossible angles. With every snap and pop, Junho's cries grew weaker, more guttural, until they resembled animalistic growls rather than human sounds. Minjay was rooted to the spot, too horrified to move, his brain desperately trying to rationalize what was unfolding.

The air in the room felt heavier, almost humid, carrying a faint, briny scent that reminded Minjay of low tide at the beach. The aroma made his stomach churn. It wasn't just Junho who had changed. The entire atmosphere of the apartment seemed alien now, oppressive.

Minjay backed away until he hit the wall. His chest heaved, his mind racing to make sense of the impossible transformation

before him. Junho was no longer Junho. He was something else now, something monstrous.

And then Junho turned to look at him.

Those black, soulless eyes locked onto Minjay, and for a moment, nothing else existed. Junho—or the creature that used to be Junho—took a halting step forward, his newly formed pincers snapping in the air.

Minjay's breath caught in his throat. "Stay back," he whispered, though his voice trembled with fear. "Junho, if you're still in there… please, stay back."

The creature paused, as if considering his words. But then it lunged.

Minjay barely had time to dive out of the way. He hit the floor hard, pain jolting through his side, but adrenaline kept him moving. He scrambled to his feet and ran for the door. His hands fumbled with the lock, shaking so badly that he almost couldn't get it open.

Behind him, he heard the sound of claws scraping against the hardwood floor. The creature—Junho—was coming for him.

Minjay threw open the door and stumbled into the hallway. He didn't stop running, didn't dare look back. He needed to get out, to find help, to…

A sharp, searing pain shot through his stomach, stopping him in his tracks. He doubled over, clutching his abdomen as the pain spread like wildfire.

"No," he gasped. "No, no, no…"

It was happening to him, too. He could feel it. The cramps, the heat, the way his skin seemed to crawl and stretch. The sensation was maddening, an itch beneath his flesh that he

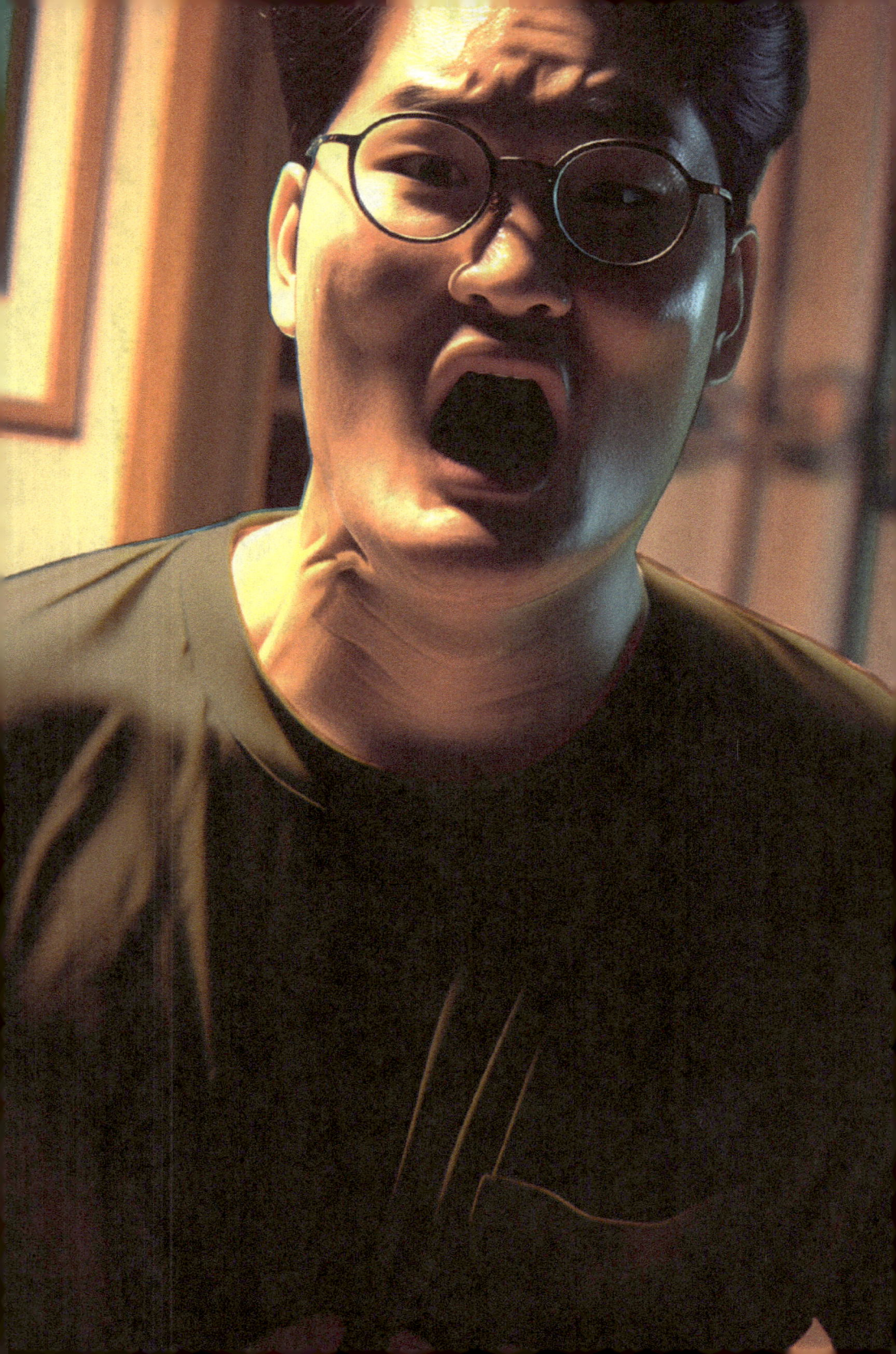

couldn't reach. He sank to his knees, tears streaming down his face as the first pincer broke through his back.

The hallway spun around him, the fluorescent lights above flickering ominously. He tried to crawl forward, but his body refused to obey. Instead, it convulsed and twisted, reshaping itself into something other, something wrong.

The seconds stretched into eternity as Minjay's body changed. His breathing grew ragged, his mind torn between fear and an inexplicable, alien hunger that gnawed at his consciousness. His vision blurred, the hallway lights fracturing into strange, unnatural shapes. He clawed at the floor, his nails splintering, until his fingers themselves began to harden, merging into the beginnings of claws.

Minjay's last coherent thought was of the crab cakes. The delicious, irresistible crab cakes. A strange, distorted thought crept into his mind, one that didn't feel entirely his own: You will feed.

Through the haze of transformation, he heard noises—footsteps, voices echoing down the hallway. Were they neighbors? Strangers who'd heard the commotion? Part of him wanted to scream for help, to warn them away. But that part was drowning, fading beneath the relentless tide of change.

The footsteps grew louder. A curious knock sounded on a nearby door, hesitant at first, then firmer. "Hello? Is everything okay in there?"

Minjay's body jerked forward involuntarily, his limbs unrecognizable. His distorted reflection in a glass cabinet caught his eye—black, glossy eyes stared back at him, devoid of humanity. The hunger swelled, insistent, pushing every other thought aside.

The door to the hallway opened slightly. A man peeked out, a middle-aged tenant Minjay vaguely recognized. "Hey, I heard—"

Minjay moved before he could think, driven by instinct. The man's scream echoed as the door slammed shut, leaving behind only muffled thuds and the wet, crunching sounds of feeding.

Down the hall, other doors creaked open. More neighbors, curious and concerned, began to step out. They wouldn't remain unaware for long.

The hunger spread like a virus, overtaking thought and reason. Minjay was no longer Minjay. He was a part of something larger, something ancient and terrible. The aroma of crab lingered, filling the air with a haunting sweetness. It was a scent that promised more than taste; it promised transformation, a call that no one in the building would escape.

The crab cakes weren't just food. They were a gateway, a catalyst. And now, the city would know their secret.

Forbidden Craft

There's a place near campus, a sorority house, that's more than it appears. The sisters there, they call it their "coven," and when I first heard that, I didn't think much of it. It was all just college superstition, right? A couple of girls with too much free time, playing pretend with witchcraft. But then I moved in, and I realized that there's always a grain of truth in every rumor.

It started off as just a house, old and full of creaking wood, with a strange kind of silence that made you think twice before you entered any room. I remember the first time I saw it—the library. The dim lighting, the way the candles seemed to flicker even when there was no wind, and the books. It was all too much. I should've left then, but curiosity got the best of me. And that's how I found myself here, alone in the house with nothing but a note that felt... wrong.

"Easter is the holiest night. Find the eggs. Perform the ritual. Prove you belong."

The words had been scribbled hastily, like they didn't want to be remembered. It was left for me when the rest of the girls went away for the holiday, a test, they said. A tradition. Every year, the sisters found a new pledge, and if the pledge could complete the ritual by midnight, they'd become part of their

"family." And if not? Well, I didn't want to think about that. I had to do it. I had to prove myself.

The map that came with the note led me to three strange locations across town. The first, an old barn on the outskirts. The second, a sewer beneath the town that smelled like wet earth and decay. And the last, a spot deep in the woods, where the trees grew so thick that even the moonlight couldn't cut through. It was all a little much, but I didn't hesitate. I'd come this far, and I wasn't going to back out now.

I grabbed my coat and slipped out into the night. The air was cold, but not cold enough to discourage me. As I walked, I couldn't shake the feeling that I wasn't alone. It wasn't the kind of feeling you get when someone's watching you—it was something deeper, more primal. Something ancient. Something that made my skin prickle.

The barn was the first stop. The door creaked as I pushed it open, the smell of dust and old straw rushing to greet me. Inside, the air was thick and musty. But there, buried under the hay, I found it. A black egg, smooth and cold in my hand. The moment I touched it, a chill ran through me, and I had to force myself to look away. The thing felt alive.

I shoved it into my bag without a second thought, moving quickly toward the next place. The sewer was worse. I felt the weight of the darkness around me, a suffocating thing that wrapped itself around my chest. The walls were slick, covered in moss, and the air was thick with mildew. I shone my flash-light down the narrow passageways, feeling like something might emerge from the shadows at any second.

That's when I found the second egg, wedged between two pipes. This one, when I touched it, felt… almost warm, like there was something inside it, something waiting. I didn't even want to look at it too closely, but I couldn't resist. I put it in my bag and ran.

The woods were the final stop. By the time I reached them, I felt like I was walking in a dream. The trees were too tall, the silence too deep. There was no wind, no sounds of animals. Just this eerie, unnatural stillness. I moved deeper into the forest, my breath shallow, my pulse quickening. When I found the final egg nestled in the hollow of an ancient oak tree, I almost couldn't believe it. This one, too, pulsed with something unknown, something... alive.

I left the woods quickly. I was afraid to stay, afraid to know what that pulsing meant. But I had to return. I had to finish this. I was almost there.

Back at the sorority house, the air felt wrong. Everything was too quiet. The house seemed to hold its breath, waiting. The library, the ritual room—it was all set up, just as the grimoire had told me. I laid the eggs in a triangle on the table, the black shells glinting ominously in the candlelight. The rabbit in the cage watched me with wide eyes, its fur soft and white, as if it didn't belong there.

The book was old, the pages fraying with age, but the symbols were clear. The words I had to speak were strange, old, and heavy. My tongue stumbled over them as I said them aloud, each one tasting foreign in my mouth. The ritual, it said, had to be performed by midnight, or else. But I wasn't going to let fear stop me.

The first egg cracked open easily, spilling a thick, black liquid onto the table. Inside was a human brain—small, pale, and slick. I quickly moved on to the second, my hands trembling. The blood, dark and sticky, poured out as I cut it open. There, inside, was a human heart, perfectly formed, still fresh and beating in the liquid. The third egg was the worst. The eyes—human eyes—gleamed up at me from the blackened liquid, wide open, staring at me like they could see everything.

The ritual was too much. I almost wanted to stop, to throw it all away, but I couldn't. I was so close. I turned to the rabbit, my

heart hammering. The grimoire instructed me to prepare its pelt, to sew the organs inside. I couldn't bring myself to look at the thing, not fully, but the instructions were clear. When I was done, the doll lay in front of me, stitched together with the bloodied organs inside. The sight of it... I can't explain it. It wasn't a doll. It wasn't a rabbit. It was something else. Something alive. I could feel it. I stepped back, laughing nervously. Was this some kind of prank? A sick joke? But the doll... it wasn't a joke.

I turned to wash my hands in the sink, trying to rid myself of the blood that clung to my skin. When I came back, the doll was gone.

The house felt different now. It wasn't just empty. It was something else entirely—alive, almost as though it had awakened from a long slumber. The air was thick with a strange heaviness, pressing in around me, wrapping around my chest like a cold, suffocating blanket. The usual hum of the house, the creaks and groans of the old wood, was gone. Instead, there was only an unnerving silence, so thick and suffocating that I could feel it pressing against my ears. It was as if the house itself was holding its breath, waiting, watching.

I tried to steady my nerves, but each step I took seemed to amplify the quiet around me. The sound of my footsteps on the old wooden floor echoed down the hallway, unnervingly loud, as if the house itself was listening to each movement. It was as if the air itself was holding its breath, waiting for me to make the next move. The blood on the floor was no longer just a strange, unsettling sight—it was now a clear, deliberate trail leading away from the table, trailing down the hallway like some sinister path that had been carefully placed for me to follow. The blood was still fresh, dark red and slick, and as I looked down at it, I couldn't help but feel that it wasn't supposed to be there. But there was no turning back now.

My heart was pounding in my chest, and I could feel my throat tightening as I took each slow, cautious step. The blood felt...

wrong. It wasn't like anything I had ever seen. There was a strange, unnatural quality to it, like it had been placed there for a reason—like it was guiding me somewhere. But where? The house was empty, wasn't it? I was alone, wasn't I?

I wasn't so sure anymore.

The blood seemed to pulse, almost as though it were alive, breathing with a rhythm that didn't belong to any human. It flowed in strange, unnatural patterns, swirling around the edges of the hallway like it had a mind of its own. I could feel my skin crawling as I walked, my eyes constantly darting around, afraid of what I might see out of the corner of my eye. The air seemed to shimmer with a low hum now, a sound so faint I couldn't quite place it, but I could feel it reverberating through the walls, through my bones.

With every step, the house seemed to grow darker, the shadows stretching further into the hall, until it felt like the light itself was being sucked into the walls. It wasn't just the lack of light— it was as though the darkness itself had come alive, creeping along the floor, pooling in corners, clinging to the edges of the room. The blood continued to lead me down the hallway, towards the staircase at the far end. My eyes were drawn to it, the trail winding up to the top, where the shadows seemed to gather, thick and impenetrable.

I stopped at the top of the stairs, my breath coming in shallow gasps. The blood trail stretched before me, now leading down into the darkened first floor. The darkness below seemed to swallow up the last remnants of light. It was as if the shadows themselves had grown hungry, pulling everything into their depths, leaving nothing behind.

The silence was absolute, but the air was full of something— something that was not right. I couldn't explain it, but every fiber of my being screamed at me to turn around and run. But I couldn't. The blood called me forward, each drop dragging me closer to the unknown. I didn't know what awaited me at the

bottom of those stairs, but I had to find out. I had to know what was pulling me deeper into the house. The weight of the silence pressed harder on my chest, but there was no turning back now. The house was alive, and I was part of it. And whatever was waiting for me down there, I had no choice but to face it.

Something wasn't right.

I crept down, the blood trail leading me into the living room. That's when I saw it. The doll. It was standing in the middle of the room, staring at me with those button eyes, the grin stitched across its face.

It was alive.

I didn't know what happened next. My feet were moving, but my mind couldn't keep up. The doll... it wasn't a doll anymore. It was something else. Something ancient. Something hungry.

I turned, desperate to escape, but no matter where I went, it was always there, waiting. The walls felt like they were closing in. The shadows, they moved, stretched. The doll's eyes never left me.

I remember the feeling of my legs giving out beneath me. The last thing I saw was the doll, stepping toward me, its grin impossibly wide. The shadows blurred around me, until everything was consumed by darkness.

When the other girls came back the next day, they found the house quiet, unnaturally still. The library, untouched. But the living room...

The doll was sitting there, smiling, waiting. Its eyes glinted, and its grin stretched wider.

And the air, thick with the scent of iron and decay, seemed to whisper with a dark promise. Something had changed. Something had awoken.

Cube Head

Tanya had always been cautious, but that night, something about the air felt different. The night was still, the kind of stillness that pressed in on her from all sides. It was the sort of quiet that made you feel like the world was holding its breath, waiting for something to break it. Even the trees seemed to be holding back their whispers, their leaves suspended in the air as if frozen. She glanced at the clock—10:42 PM. Later than usual for her walk with Max, her fluffy, cheerful dog. But Max didn't seem to mind. He bounced eagerly at her side, as though the hour meant nothing. She tucked her jacket tighter around her shoulders and stepped into the night, the crisp air biting at her skin.

The suburban neighborhood around her was unnervingly quiet. The usual hum of distant cars, the occasional laugh or murmur from nearby houses—none of that was present. The silence pressed on her, thick and suffocating. The only sound was the soft shuffle of Tanya's sneakers crunching over gravel as she walked along the alley behind the row of houses. Max trotted ahead of her, his tail wagging furiously as he bounded from side to side, oblivious to the growing unease that gnawed at Tanya.

The alleyway was familiar—too familiar. She had taken this path countless times before, but tonight, it felt different. The

path wound through the backs of the houses, past overgrown fences and darkened windows, a shortcut to the park on the other side of the neighborhood. She told herself it was just the hour, the strange quiet, but something deep in her gut told her otherwise.

Halfway down the alley, Max suddenly stopped. His nose twitched, his ears perked. The change in his demeanor was instant, and Tanya felt a cold ripple of unease wash over her. His body stiffened, and for the first time that evening, Max wasn't bouncing or wagging his tail. He was still—rigid, like a statue. Tanya instinctively slowed her pace, her eyes scanning the shadows ahead, trying to discern what had caught his attention.

Max's tail flicked once, twice. Then he bolted.

Without warning, Max tore off, his leash slipping from Tanya's fingers in an instant. "Max!" she shouted, panic rising in her chest as she chased after him. He was faster than she'd ever seen him before, darting through the darkness like a ghost, vanishing around the corner of the alley. Tanya's heart raced as she sprinted after him, the sound of her breath harsh and quick in her ears. The only light came from a distant porch, barely illuminating the path ahead. It felt as though the night had swallowed everything else up—swallowed her, too.

Tanya rounded the corner, her phone's flashlight shaking in her hand as she desperately tried to keep the beam steady. She found Max at the far end of the alley, pawing at something hidden behind a tangle of overgrown bushes. At first, she thought it was just another animal, a stray cat or a raccoon. But then the sound came—a low, guttural, wet noise that made Tanya's stomach lurch in discomfort. It wasn't an animal.

"Max," Tanya called again, her voice cracking. She took a step forward, the light from her phone trembling in her hand as she crept closer. The noise stopped, and Max let out a sharp whine, followed by an eerie yelp before he disappeared into the

shadows. Tanya's breath caught in her throat as she lunged forward, the flashlight beam flickering wildly in the night. She froze when the light landed on a dark, glistening puddle at her feet. Blood.

Her stomach churned. She scanned the area with frantic eyes. "Max?" she whispered, her voice barely a breath. She had no idea what had happened, but she knew she didn't want to find out. Her heart pounded in her chest, too loud, too fast, drowning out everything else. There was no sign of Max. Not a trace of him except the blood. The smear of crimson disappeared into the shadows, leading her further down the alley, toward something that felt far too wrong. Then, she heard it again.

A soft, rhythmic clicking, like fingernails tapping against glass. So faint, she almost missed it, like the faint echo of a distant, forgotten sound. It seemed to come from just beyond the pool of blood, beyond the bushes that swayed gently in the still air. Tanya's fingers tightened around the phone, her palms slick with sweat as she aimed the flashlight in the direction of the noise. And then she saw it.

A figure standing motionless among the foliage. At first, Tanya thought it was a mannequin—an odd thing to find in the dark, but not impossible. The figure was tall, draped in a flowing white gown that rippled slightly, despite the absence of any wind. But it wasn't the gown that made Tanya's heart stop—it was the head. The head was a perfect white cube, smooth and featureless. At first glance, it looked like a block of marble, but the longer she stared, the more she felt something was wrong. Something was deeply wrong.

The face was carved into the surface of the cube. A human face, yet distorted—wrong. The features were too smooth, too perfect, as though they had been molded from memory, but with all the finer details forgotten. The eyes were deep-set, hollow, and the mouth was twisted into an almost-smile, but it didn't reach the gaze. It was a smile that didn't belong, a smile that made her stomach churn with a sudden, visceral sense of terror.

Tanya's legs locked. She couldn't move, couldn't even breathe properly. Her heart thudded against her ribs, each beat louder than the last. She stood frozen, caught between the overwhelming urge to run and the strange paralysis that held her in place. Her breath came in short, sharp gasps. The clicking sound grew louder, more insistent, its rhythm drilling into her skull like nails on glass.

The cube's mouth opened, and the voice emerged. It was low, layered with something unsettling, like a thousand voices merging into one, all at once.

"Lost…" it whispered, the word stretching unnaturally in the air. "Why are you… lost?"

Tanya's mind scrambled for an explanation, but nothing made sense. The words burrowed into her mind, digging past the logical thoughts and unsettling her with their presence. It wasn't a question that made sense—it shouldn't have mattered, yet it felt like a knife in her brain. The darkness around her seemed to thicken, the air heavier, suffocating. She felt like she was drowning in it.

"Lost…" the figure repeated, the voice now richer, deeper, reverberating through her bones, rattling her insides. Her fingers twitched as she reached into her pocket. Slowly, her hand wrapped around the stun gun her brother had insisted she carry. The small, pink device felt oddly cold against her clammy palm. She pulled it out, her hands shaking, and her thumb hovered over the trigger. "Stay back," she whispered, her voice barely a breath. The words felt fragile in her throat, but they were all she had left.

The figure tilted its head, an unnatural, mechanical movement. The motion was smooth, too smooth, like the thing wasn't really there at all. It was as though it was controlled by strings that Tanya couldn't see, a puppet in a dance she couldn't understand. The figure took a slow, deliberate step forward, and Tanya's heart seized in her chest. The white gown glided over

the ground without a sound, as though the figure wasn't even touching the earth.

"Lost..." it repeated, the voice now deeper, more resonant. The hum in the air grew louder, vibrating through her chest, through her bones. It felt like the world itself was about to crack under the weight of it. Tanya tightened her grip on the stun gun, her knuckles white. She stepped backward, her breath coming in shallow gasps. Every fiber of her being screamed for her to run, but she couldn't move. The cube's hollow eyes seemed to fix on her, or was it just her imagination? She couldn't tell, but it felt as though it saw right through her, as though it knew everything she had ever feared.

The figure stepped forward again, its movements almost fluid, gliding like a shadow. Tanya's legs finally obeyed her, but only for a split second. She lunged forward, pressing the stun gun against the figure's arm, and pulled the trigger. The crackling surge of electricity was deafening, filling the alley with a bright flash of light.

For a moment, the figure convulsed, jerking violently, its limbs twisting in strange angles. The hum escalated into an ear-splitting shriek that made Tanya cover her ears, the pitch unbearable. Then, the cube's surface began to warp. The smooth edges stretched, flickering between solid and liquid, as if it was being pulled apart. Its carved face contorted, the expression—what was it? Pain? Rage?—twisting unnaturally. The gown collapsed inward, folding like fabric caught in a vacuum. Tanya stumbled backward, her legs buckling beneath her. The figure's body crumpled into a pile of white fabric, its shape folding in on itself. But the cube's head hovered above the mess, spinning slowly, its edges flickering like static on an old TV. The face remained, a grimace frozen in place.

Tanya's breath caught in her throat as the cube's hollow eyes seemed to narrow, locking onto her. The world seemed to stop, suspended in the tense air. Then, with a soft, nauseating pop, the figure vanished. Silence. Tanya stood, gasping, her mind

struggling to understand what she had just seen. Her hands shook violently, dropping the stun gun to the ground. She looked at the pile of fabric, the white robe that lay crumpled on the ground, as ordinary as any other piece of clothing. It didn't belong. It couldn't. Max was gone—vanished without a trace, without a single paw print leading away from the scene.

With shaky steps, Tanya backed away. Her stomach churned as she tried to process what had happened. The robe. The blood. The creature. It didn't make sense. Nothing made sense. She glanced at the spot where the figure had been—nothing remained, just the quiet, eerie stillness. Max was gone.

Tanya returned home that night in a daze, locking every door and window with trembling hands. She sat on her bed, staring at the wall, the events replaying in her mind like a broken record. The legend of Cube Head—the stories, the whispers—she had always thought it was just a myth. A silly legend passed around by kids at sleepovers and online forums. But now... now she knew. Myths don't leave behind bloodstains and empty robes.

In the days that followed, Tanya avoided the alley. She stayed on well-lit streets, sticking to the crowds of people and the safety of public spaces. She told no one about what had happened—afraid of their questions, their disbelief. The memory of that night lingered in the back of her mind, a dark shadow she couldn't escape. Every time she closed her eyes, she saw the hollow eyes of that carved face, the smooth white cube tilting ever so slightly, whispering its terrible question.

"Why are you... lost?"

Iron Lung

Piper stood at the back of the church, watching as the coffin that held her late grandfather was lowered into the ground. She felt a weight settle in her chest, but it wasn't grief. Not entirely. There was something else.

A gnawing sense of unease that had been present ever since his passing, a suspicion that had only grown stronger in the hours following the funeral. Her grandpa's death had never quite made sense to her.

It hadn't been an accident or a natural cause, no matter how the authorities had explained it. Something was off, and she couldn't shake the feeling that the truth was buried just beneath the surface.

When the service ended and the mourners dispersed, Piper took her time leaving. She had one more thing to do before she could allow herself to mourn properly. There were items her grandfather had specifically requested for her to have after his death. A few keepsakes. A key. A card. A journal.

When the last of the funeral goers had trickled out of the graveyard, Piper made her way back to her grandfather's house. The place felt hollow, abandoned, as if it hadn't been lived in for

years, even though she knew it had only been a few days since his death.

The house was old, but not in a charming way. It was too large for just the two of them, its rooms filled with shadows, with the faintest echo of creaking wood. It was the kind of house that made you feel like you were being watched, even when you were alone.

She unlocked the door and stepped inside. The silence swallowed her whole, amplifying the thudding of her own heartbeat in her chest.

Her grandpa's things were still where they had always been, but there was something...wrong. Something that crawled under her skin, a sense of unease that prickled the back of her neck.

She didn't let it stop her, though. Her grandpa had been a man of meticulous order, and he had a way of making sure that everything was taken care of, even after his death. He'd left her a set of instructions. At least, that's what she thought. It had to be. She was his only heir.

Piper moved cautiously into the living room, her eyes immediately drawn to the corner. There, in the middle of the room, stood the iron lung.

It had been there for as long as she could remember. Her grandfather had spent his last years in it, trapped inside its metal walls, only able to breathe thanks to the mechanical assistance it provided. It was a symbol of his suffering, a reminder of the frailty of life.

Yet now, standing in the room, Piper couldn't shake the feeling that it was more than just a relic of her grandfather's illness. It felt...alive.

Her heart began to race. There was something wrong with it, something that shouldn't be there.

She walked closer, drawn inexplicably to the machine. As she reached out to touch it, a sudden chill ran through her, as if a breeze had swept through the room.

She recoiled, but before she could pull her hand back, the iron lung shuddered. It rattled in place, its old metal frame creaking as though it were waking from a long sleep. The sound was faint at first, a low hum that seemed to vibrate through her chest. But then it grew louder.

Her breath hitched in her throat. Was it…breathing?

Piper took a step back. This wasn't normal. Her grandfather had died in that thing. There should have been nothing left of it—no strange hum, no movement. But the iron lung seemed to be shifting, responding to something.

A faint whisper echoed in her ears, almost imperceptible. Was it the wind? No. It was something else.

Piper hesitated for only a moment before she pulled herself together. She wasn't the type to let fear control her. She was a journalist—a seeker of truth. And if there was something in this house, something tied to her grandfather's death, she was going to find it.

She hurried through the house, searching for any clue, anything that might shed light on what had happened. Her footsteps echoed in the hallways, amplifying the growing sense of dread that clung to the house.

In the study, she finally found what she was looking for—a small wooden box hidden among her grandfather's papers. It was locked, but she was quick to use the key she had found earlier, her fingers trembling with anticipation as the box creaked open.

Inside, there was a red journal. It was old, the leather cover cracked with age. The pages inside were yellowed, the ink faded, but there was something chilling about it all the same. The journal didn't belong to her grandfather. It was her grandmother's.

Piper's fingers brushed over the cover, and a shiver ran down her spine. She had never seen her grandmother's handwriting before, never even heard her speak.

Her grandfather had always told her that his wife, Margaret, had died years before they'd met. But this...this was something else.

The journal wasn't just a keepsake—it was a clue.

Her mind raced as she skimmed through the pages, her eyes scanning the words for any hint of what had happened in the final days of her grandfather's life.

There were strange notes, cryptic phrases. At one point, she read something that sent a chill through her: "He doesn't know. He doesn't know what I've done. But he will soon enough."

Piper's breath caught in her throat. Margaret. The widow. Had she been involved in her grandfather's death?

Before she could process it further, a sound from the driveway caught her attention. The unmistakable screech of tires on gravel. Margaret was home.

Panic surged through Piper's veins. She needed to get out of there—needed to get the journal into the hands of the police. But the door creaked open, and Margaret's voice echoed through the house.

"I'm home, Piper. I'll be upstairs in a moment."

Piper's heart raced as she grabbed the journal and shoved it into her bag. She turned to run, but as she did, she stumbled. A cold hand brushed against her shoulder, and she spun around, her fists raised.

Margaret was standing there, her eyes cold and calculating. The older woman's lips twisted into a smile, but there was something wrong about it. The kind of smile you give when you know something someone else doesn't.

"You're not leaving this house with that," Margaret hissed.

Before Piper could react, Margaret lunged. The fight was over quickly. Margaret was stronger than she looked, but Piper was quick. She knocked her down, stumbling backward in the chaos, heart racing in her chest. The house felt alive now, as if the walls themselves were closing in.

The sound of sirens in the distance grew louder. Margaret scrambled to her feet, her face twisted in anger, but Piper didn't give her another chance. She darted for the door, just as the first police car pulled into the driveway.

Piper sat in the interrogation room, her fingers twitching nervously as she recounted the events to the officers. She told them everything—well, almost everything. She left out the supernatural aspects. The iron lung. The whispers. The way the house had felt like it was watching her. It was too much. She wasn't sure how much of it had been real.

The officers seemed skeptical, but they took the journal. They promised to look into it. The questions they asked were routine, and Piper answered them the best she could.

When they left, she returned to the living room, her eyes drawn once again to the iron lung. She wasn't sure what she was expecting, but she had to know. Was her grandfather's soul still trapped inside it? Could he communicate with her?

She moved toward the machine, her breath shallow. She knelt down beside it, closing her eyes for a moment as she reached out to touch it.

A faint voice echoed in her mind, a soft whisper that felt like it was coming from the very walls of the house.

"Piper," the voice said. "Help me."

Her eyes snapped open. The room felt colder. The air grew thick. But there was something else now—something dark, something ancient. And then, for just a moment, Piper thought she saw a figure standing in the window.

She wasn't alone.

The investigation had only just begun.

Prankster Peter

Lionel had lived alone for years. The house was old, creaking under its age, filled with memories of days long past. The wallpaper sagged, peeling at the edges. The floors groaned with each step, the foundation feeling as though it were gradually sinking deeper into the earth. For years, Lionel had grown accustomed to the silence of the house—comforted by its familiar emptiness. The house had become his companion, though it was a companion that came with its own sense of suffocating loneliness. It was a place where time moved slowly, and the outside world felt like a distant echo.

But then came the shadow.

It began subtly, like a trick of the light. Lionel thought nothing of it at first. A shape in the corner of his eye, fleeting and indistinct, vanishing the moment he tried to focus. He was no stranger to such oddities—old houses had a way of playing with your senses. The creaking of the wood, the drafty hallways, the occasional cold spot. But as the days passed, the shadow grew more persistent. It was always there, hanging in the corners, shifting when he wasn't looking. Always watching. Always waiting.

It wasn't long before Lionel began to see it in more detail—tall, impossibly tall, its form draped in a flowing black veil. The veil

was so dark it seemed to absorb the light, shifting in an unsettling way, like the very fabric of it was alive. Beneath the veil, there were no distinct features—only an impression of a shape, of something looming, its presence a thick, oppressive weight in the room. But the worst part was the eyes—or the lack thereof. The thing didn't need eyes to make its gaze felt. Lionel could feel it, always, in the back of his mind.

It wasn't long before the entity began to speak.

"Are you lonely, Lionel?" The voice was soft, almost sweet, though there was something about it that made Lionel's skin crawl. It wasn't a whisper—no, it was too clear for that—but it wasn't full of malice either. It was more like a playful murmur, an invitation to something darker.

"You don't have to be alone, Lionel. I could keep you company... forever."

That's when he first saw it clearly—its head tilted unnaturally, its veil moving like it was part of the air itself. A face, indistinct beneath the veil, but the shape of it was wrong, like it wasn't meant to be seen. The creature wasn't just haunting him. It was taunting him.

It didn't have a name at first, but soon Lionel found himself calling it Peter, for lack of anything better. The name felt fitting somehow, like it had always belonged to the creature. Peter never made a sound unless he wanted to. But when he did, his voice was laced with a mocking sweetness that made Lionel's insides twist with unease.

"You have a weak heart, don't you, Lionel?" Peter's voice would float through the air, a faint chuckle in his tone. "A pacemaker, I think? You shouldn't be here, all alone. It's dangerous."

The first time Lionel felt the weight of Peter's presence, it made his chest tighten. He reached for his pacemaker as though it might suddenly stop working, as though Peter's voice was

enough to make his heart skip a beat. Peter was everywhere. He appeared when Lionel least expected it—always watching, always waiting, sometimes in the corners of the room, sometimes in the shadows behind him, and occasionally, right in front of him.

One moment Peter would be a distant silhouette, looming near the ceiling, and the next, he'd be standing just inches from Lionel, his black veil swirling like smoke, obscuring whatever horrors lay beneath. He would stand there, still and silent, and stare at Lionel with that sickening presence.

The thing wasn't just a figment of his imagination. It was real.

Peter's hauntings grew worse over time. It wasn't just the looming presence, the voice that never left. Peter started playing cruel games with Lionel. Sometimes, when Lionel would walk through the rooms, he'd hear the soft rustling of fabric behind him. He'd turn quickly, but Peter was always gone. But Lionel could feel him—always there, always just behind him. At night, when Lionel lay in bed, the silence of the house would be shattered by the faintest sound of movement. He'd open his eyes, only to find Peter standing there, staring down at him from the edge of his bed, his veil almost touching the floor.

It became a cruel routine. Peter never attacked directly. He never had to. His presence alone was enough to make Lionel's heart race, to make him wonder if he might die of fear alone. The voice would return at the worst moments, like a whisper in the dark. "You don't have much time left, Lionel. Come with me. I can make it easier for you."

Sometimes, Lionel would hear Peter laughing softly, almost as if he was enjoying the fear he inspired.

It wasn't long before Lionel's sleep, already shattered by his age and illness, became nonexistent. He couldn't sleep knowing Peter was lurking, waiting for the right moment to make his

presence known. The silence between Peter's appearances was only filled with dread. But after a week of this torment, Lionel realized something: Peter appeared with a pattern. He showed up once an hour, without fail. That knowledge gave Lionel some semblance of control, or at least the illusion of it. He started setting an alarm clock, using it as a way to regulate his fear, to make sure he was awake when Peter returned. It wasn't much, but it was something to hold onto.

Every time the alarm went off, Lionel's mind would race. He would try to busy himself—washing dishes, pacing around the house, anything to avoid the corners, the dark spots where Peter liked to appear. His eyes would flicker toward the walls, the floorboards, searching for that veil. Every creak, every whisper in the house felt like a signal, a reminder that Peter was always there, always near.

And then one night, it happened.

Lionel was woken from a fitful sleep by an icy chill that shot up his spine, freezing him to his bones. It wasn't the cold—it was something far worse.

It was a sensation that didn't belong. It was as if something had entered his body, sliding beneath his skin, sinking into his very soul. His eyes snapped open, and there, standing above him, was Peter.

Only now, the figure wasn't just watching him. It was inside him. Peter was angry. The crackling sound—the same sound that always filled the room when Peter was near—was louder now, sharper. It vibrated through Lionel's entire body. Peter seemed to be feeding off his fear, feeding off the terror in his eyes.

"Your heart can't take this much longer, Lionel," Peter hissed. "You should join me. Come with me, and you won't have to feel this anymore."

The words cut through Lionel like a knife. He could feel his heart pounding in his chest, a relentless beat that echoed in his ears. But something in him snapped. No. He couldn't take it anymore. He was done being afraid. Done with Peter's games.

With trembling hands, Lionel stumbled to the garage. He couldn't think clearly—only that he needed to fight back. He didn't care about the state of his heart or the risk it posed.

He grabbed the wood axe, the one that had sat unused for years, and raised it above his head. His heart hammered, but this time, it wasn't out of fear. It was out of resolve. He had to do something.

Lionel swung the axe into the wall, his breath ragged, his heart pounding. The first strike barely made a mark, but Lionel didn't stop. He swung again, and again. Each blow felt like a victory, like he was striking back against the thing that had tormented him for so long.

Sweat poured down his face as he swung harder, the axe biting into the wall. He could feel his heart racing, but he was too far gone now to stop. The walls cracked and groaned, and Lionel continued until the hole was wide enough to reveal the hidden room behind it.

Inside, in the center of the room, was a single brick that glowed with an eerie, faint light. It radiated warmth, its surface slick with a strange energy. The crackling sound—the same noise that Peter always made—seemed to come from the very brick itself. Lionel knew this was the source. This was the heart of Peter's curse.

He wasted no time. The axe came down on the glowing brick with a crack. The moment it struck, a burst of light exploded from the brick, sending a wave of heat through the room. Sparks of supernatural energy flew from the impact, showering the room in a blaze of unnatural light. It felt like the very air was vibrating with power.

Lionel swung again, this time with more force, his eyes wide as the crackling intensified. Each strike sent another burst of bright, fiery energy, sharp and painful. The brick began to fracture, the supernatural sparks flying faster, more violently. Finally, with a final, mighty blow, the brick shattered into pieces, releasing a sharp scream that echoed through the house—Peter's scream.

The room grew silent. The presence, the weight of Peter's existence, was gone.

But as Lionel stood there, panting, his heart still thundering in his chest, the eerie silence seemed wrong. It wasn't peaceful—it was hollow. He had destroyed the source, but the questions that followed were still there, lingering like a dark shadow.

Who had placed the brick in the wall? And why had it been there, pulsing with dark power?

As the house seemed to exhale, Lionel knew one thing for certain: Peter was gone—but something else, something far worse, might still be lurking beneath the surface.

VintaVision

Joe had always been fascinated by oddities, and Sterling's Emporium of Oddities had a magnetic pull on him, one he couldn't resist. The shop was tucked away in a forgotten corner of the city, its blinking neon sign fighting against the rain-soaked evening. The more Joe tried to ignore it, the more it drew him in.

The door creaked as he entered, the bell above it jingling faintly. The air inside was thick, carrying a scent he couldn't place—something earthy, metallic, and faintly sweet, like the remnants of forgotten history. The shelves were cluttered with strange trinkets, each one out of place in the modern world: tarnished clocks, cracked porcelain dolls, and objects that had no clear purpose. They filled the room like misplaced memories, whispering of stories that never should have been told.

As Joe wandered deeper into the shop, his eyes caught something strange, something that didn't belong amidst the chaos of forgotten relics: a remote control sitting on the counter. At first, it seemed entirely ordinary—green plastic, worn buttons, the kind of thing you'd find discarded in an old drawer. But as he stepped closer, his eyes narrowed. The symbols on the buttons were odd—swirling, intricate shapes that made his head ache the longer he stared at them. They weren't numbers

or letters. They were something else. He reached out, but before he could touch it, a voice emerged from the shadows.

"That's no ordinary remote."

Joe jumped, turning to see Sterling stepping out from the dim corners of the shop. His wiry frame was almost unnaturally thin, his sharp eyes gleaming under the harsh fluorescent lights that buzzed above. The shopkeeper seemed too vivid against the dim backdrop of the room, a figure more fitting for a nightmare than a dusty shop.

"It's a universal controller," Sterling continued, his voice rasping like old paper. "Works on every television ever made... and some you've never even heard of."

Joe raised an eyebrow. "What does that mean?"

Sterling's lips curled into a thin smile. "It'll show you things you can't find anywhere else. Unique programming," he said, his eyes locking onto Joe's with unnerving intensity. "But remember, all sales are final."

Joe hesitated, but the pull of curiosity was stronger than his doubts. He paid for the remote, the weight of it strangely satisfying in his palm, heavier than it seemed. He felt as though something was about to change, something that had already been set into motion, but he couldn't quite place why.

That night, after the rain had begun tapping a steady rhythm against his window, Joe sat down on the couch and pointed the remote at his television. His fingers hovered over the buttons. A nervous excitement coursed through him. He pressed the power button.

At first, nothing happened. The screen flickered, then shifted. The black-and-white world on the screen bled slowly into color. At first, it was subtle—the faintest hint of warmth creeping into the edges of the tablecloth, a glint of gold in a picture frame

hanging crookedly on the wall. But then the colors deepened, saturating the scene with an unsettling vibrancy. The wallpaper behind the man and woman on the screen turned a sickly, nauseating shade of green. The plates on the table began to gleam with a greasy, unnatural sheen. Even their eyes—once lifeless and dull—now gleamed with an eerie, predatory bright- ness that sent a cold shiver down Joe's spine.

The scene before him looked like it came straight out of a 1950s sitcom. A man and a woman sat at a modest kitchen table, smiling at each other. The set was meticulously detailed: patterned wallpaper, a rotary phone mounted on the wall, and a pie cooling on the windowsill. But something was off. Their smiles were too wide, their movements too stiff, too practiced. It was as if they were nothing more than puppets, controlled by invisible strings.

Suddenly, their heads turned—in unison, too smoothly—to face the camera. No, not the camera. They turned to face Joe. A jolt of panic shot through him. Their glassy eyes locked onto his, unblinking and far too aware. Joe's breath caught in his throat. His thumb fumbled over the remote as he hastily pressed the button to switch the channel.

The screen flickered, and another scene appeared. The same man and woman were now in a living room. The man stood by a mantle, adjusting a clock. The woman sat on a floral-pat- terned sofa, knitting. But once again, their heads turned, their eyes piercing Joe's, following his every movement. He switched the channel again, and again.

No matter where he went, they were always there. Their smiles stretched wider, their gazes growing sharper, more piercing, as if they were drawing closer with every passing second. A low hum began to emanate from the remote. Joe noticed a red button that hadn't been there before. It pulsed, like a heartbeat, almost as if it were calling to him.

Before he could stop himself, his thumb pressed it.

The room around him spun, the world disintegrating into static. A deafening, droning hum filled his ears, and his vision was swallowed by an oppressive darkness. Then, the static cleared, and when Joe opened his eyes, he wasn't on his couch anymore.

The air was thick and musty, heavy with the scent of decay. Joe stood in a dimly lit dining room. The walls were covered in peeling, yellowed wallpaper. A mismatched table stood before him, its surface covered in plates, each holding strips of what appeared to be dried meat. His stomach lurched.

Across from him sat the man and woman from the television. Up close, their waxy skin looked even more unnatural, and their features were unnervingly smooth—too smooth. Their eyes never left him, their smiles frozen in place, as if mocking him with their lifeless, perfect faces.

In the center of the table, there was a bust of an old woman. Her gaunt, hollow face was eerily similar to the woman at the table. Her dried, brittle features resembled the strips of meat on the plates before them. The thought of it made Joe's stomach twist in disgust.

"Welcome," the man said, his voice smooth, yet carrying an undercurrent of menace. "We've been expecting you."

Joe's heart pounded in his chest. His throat went dry. "What is this?" he whispered, his voice barely audible. The man's smile never wavered. "This is supper," he said, gesturing to the plates. "Please, sit."

Joe's legs moved of their own accord, dragging him to the empty chair at the table. He sank into it, his body heavy, his mind racing. The woman's eyes never left him, her expression disturbingly serene, as though she was patiently waiting for him to join them.

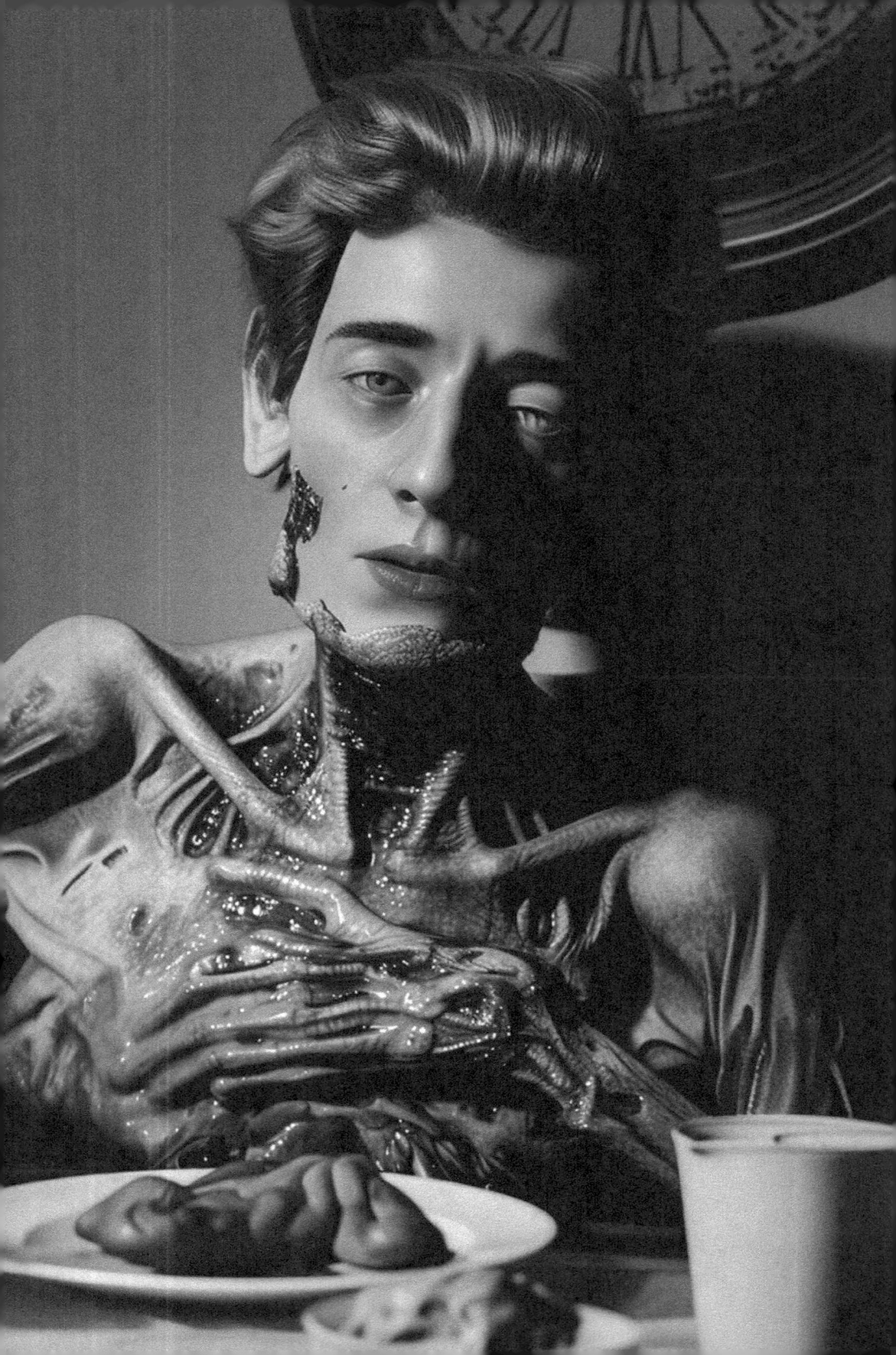

"I... I need to use the bathroom," Joe stammered, his voice shaky. Every muscle in his body screamed for him to escape, but he couldn't move.

The woman tilted her head, her smile faltering ever so slightly. "Bathroom?" she repeated, her voice hollow, confused. "What's a bathroom?"

Joe's breath caught in his throat. He swallowed hard and forced himself to speak. "It's... a private room. For cleaning up."

The woman turned to the man. "Do we need one of those?"

The man chuckled, a low, guttural sound that sent chills down Joe's spine. "No," he said, his gaze flicking back to Joe. "But you're welcome to explain it more. I do enjoy a good conversation."

Joe's fingers twitched under the table. His eyes darted to the floor, where the remote lay just out of reach. He couldn't remember dropping it, but there it was, lying on the floor next to his chair. The man's eyes followed his gaze, a smirk tugging at his lips.

"Looking for something?" the man asked, his voice darkening. "You won't be leaving, you know."

Joe's breath quickened, panic rising in his chest. The air in the room seemed to thicken with every passing second. His mind raced as he tried to come up with a plan. The bust of the old woman at the center of the table seemed to be watching him now, its hollow eyes fixed on him, tracking every movement.

"Why are you doing this?" Joe blurted out, his voice cracking under the weight of his fear. "What do you want from me?"

The man leaned forward, his grin stretching unnaturally wide. "You're part of the program now," he said, his voice dripping with something darker. "A special guest appearance."

Joe's stomach churned as the truth sank in. They weren't just watching him. They wanted him to stay. They wanted him to become part of their twisted reality. The thought of being trapped here forever sent a jolt of terror through him.

The world around Joe distorted as the room seemed to close in on him, his mind spinning, drowning in static. He tried to scream, but the sound was lost in the hum that filled the air. The figures of the man and woman loomed closer, their eyes burning with an unnatural intensity.

And then, everything went still.

Joe's body froze, his vision locked on the smiling faces of the man and woman. His skin grew taut, as if it were stretching across brittle bones. His limbs refused to move, his mouth unable to utter a single word. He was caught—completely, irreversibly trapped within the confines of the show. There was no escape. No return.

Time had no meaning here.

The static on the screen blared louder, surrounding him. His face, now grotesque and dried, stared back at him from the image on the television. His eyes were wide with terror, his flesh shriveled and desiccated, a horrific mockery of his former self. The show had consumed him entirely.

Outside, in the silence of his living room, the remote lay forgotten, a faint glow emanating from its tiny screen. On it, the same video of Joe's decayed face looped endlessly. His horrified expression remained frozen, a warning to anyone who dared to come across it.

Joe was gone.

The show had him now.

www.ingramcontent.com/pod-product-compliance
Lightning Source LLC
Chambersburg PA
CBHW072031170626
46811CB00008B/3026